MW01004176

SO YOU WANT TO BE A

SHAMAN

DAVID LAWSON

CONARI PRESS
Berkeley, CA

This book is dedicated to all of my medicine sisters who transform the world with their healing arts: Celia, Star, Kitty, Louise, Rebecca, Sasha, Stephanie, Mary, Lynne, Viv, and especially my dear friend Francesca Montaldi. In addition, I would like to thank the following people for their help in the production of this book: Susan Mears, Debbie Thorpe, Peter Bridgewater, Anne O'Rorke and Justin Carson.

Text © 1996 *David Lawson*

Originally published by Godsfield Press 1996

DESIGNED AND PRODUCED BY
THE BRIDGEWATER BOOK COMPANY LIMITED

All Rights Reserved. No part of this book may be used or reproduced in any manner whatsoever without written permission, except in the case of brief quotations in critical articles or reviews.

For information, contact:
Conari Press,
2550 Ninth St., Suite 101,
Berkeley, CA 94710

Printed and bound in Singapore

Conari Press books are distributed by Publishers Group West.

ISBN 1-57324-031-1

The publishers would like to thank the following for the use of pictures:
ARCHIV FÜR KUNST UND GESCHICHTE, London: p.2. BRIDGEMAN ART LIBRARY, London: Christie's, London p.13; Musée des Beaux-arts, Rouen/Giraudon pp.14, 29; Musée Gustave Moreau, Paris p.47. E.T. ARCHIVE: Biblioteca Marciana, Venice pp.40–41. IMAGES COLOUR LIBRARY: pp.16–17, 38 (James Thorn), 58–59, 60–61. MARY EVANS PICTURE LIBRARY: pp.9, 15, 18. RANGE/BETTMANN: p.35. SOTHEBY'S TRANSPARENCY LIBRARY: pp. 43, 64. WERNER FORMAN ARCHIVE: Provincial Museum, Victoria, British Columbia, Canada, Museum No. 1564 p.33.

For details of books, audio tapes, courses and events by the author, David Lawson, please write to Healing Workshops, P.O. Box 1678, London, NW5 4EW, U.K.

CONTENTS

INTRODUCTION

The modern world is full of miracles. Modern transportation systems can take us from our homes to the opposite side of the world in a day, medical science can cure conditions that would have been considered fatal a short time ago, and information technology allows many people rapid access to knowledge. In the face of these modern miracles, human needs and desires seem to grow rather than diminish. The need to find a greater meaning to life is stronger than ever and a fascination with the mysteries of the world inspires many to explore a multitude of spiritual paths and traditions.

Look to nature for inspiration.

Many of us wish to create lives that will make a difference to the world. Perhaps this is one reason why more and more people are drawn to some aspect of the healing arts or find jobs that serve the wellbeing of others. Within the technology and busyness that surrounds us, the spirit of the shaman is strong and well.

Herbs are central to the healing arts.

A shaman is a person who learns, through a respect and mastery of his or her own nature, to build bridges

between the physical world that we see around us and the subtle forces of the non-physical worlds that we also inhabit. Shamans develop an awareness of the spiritual nature within all things and use that awareness to serve others, bringing balance, wisdom, inspiration, education, enlightenment, and healing into the lives of other people.

Traditionally the role of shaman was given to a few chosen individuals, but in the modern world the need for shamanic awareness has grown. The ability to be a shaman is a gift that is available to everyone. There is a choice that we can all make to awaken our own unique shamanic potential.

Seek out the spiritual in all things.

WHAT IS A SHAMAN?

A shaman is a person of wisdom who uses his or her unique awareness to guide and serve others. Shamans are said to have the ability to transform energy. They develop a special knowledge of the spiritual essence within all things and are able to utilize that knowledge to create balance and harmony in the world around them.

THE ORIGINS OF THE SHAMAN

The word "shaman" may have come from the Tunguso-Manchurian word *Saman*, meaning he (or she) who knows. The Tungus peoples were originally nomadic and semi-nomadic hunters and fishermen who lived in the sub-arctic forests of eastern Siberia. Over time, the influence of other races, and of the Russian revolution, molded the Tungus into settled communities of farmers and industrial workers.

Traditionally the Tungus peoples lived in clans, each with its own shaman who was central to its religious beliefs and practices. Within these communities the shaman was a prophetic figure who used music, mediumship, and a variety of healing skills to minister to others.

Shamans leading a ceremony in a Tungus clan,
in the nineteenth century.

THE SHAMANIC WORLD

The existence and purpose of the shaman is not limited to one area of the planet or to one race of people. Shamanism in its many forms has been linked with the religious customs of numerous cultures, from pre-civilized society to the present day. In modern times, great attention has been placed upon the shamanic traditions practiced by the indigenous peoples of North and Central America, but there are also shamanistic customs to be found amongst the indigenous peoples of Africa, India, Australia, and throughout the world.

THE SPIRIT OF THE SHAMAN

The shaman has many faces and many names: in some cultures the shaman was the medicine man or medicine woman, in others the priest or priestess. Shamans do not necessarily all look the same; some are unrecognizable as such at first glance and each has his or her own unique style or expression. It is underneath the many faces, black, white, brown, olive, yellow, and red, that the true nature of the shaman lives. It is not the role, task, or job that marks the shaman but it is the motivation behind the many roles that brings the truth of shamanic awareness. For those who have eyes to see, it is possible to peel away the mask and recognize the spirit of the shaman within.

Look behind the shaman's mask.

WHO ARE THE SHAMANS?

Shamans are ordinary people with extraordinary wisdom and insight. There is a measure of shamanic wisdom within us all. The shamans are those of us who are willing to harness that inner wisdom; nurturing it like a precious seed until it has grown into a tall tree, strong and secure. The spirit of the shaman moves like the wind to animate the leaves and branches of that tree. The shaman is someone who is willing to combine his or her human strengths and weaknesses with the breath of the divine.

The shaman is the wise man, the wise woman, the mystic, the healer, the seer, the teacher, and the peacemaker. Shamans can be performers, actors, musicians, artists, naturalists, environmentalists, or negotiators. Shamans work in the world to raise the consciousness of others, activate positive change, and bring about spiritual growth for us all.

Innate wisdom has to be nurtured.

SHAMANIC FACES

Shamans are both born and created. In all cases there has been an underlying spiritual choice that each person has made to awaken his or her shamanic awareness. For some children the aura of the shaman shines out from them even before they take their first breath. Have you ever looked into the eyes of a small child and seen extraordinary wisdom radiating from within? Some shamans are born into a role or lifestyle that is indicative of their special awareness and ability. In some cultures children are recognized as the incarnations of wise or divine souls and are trained and nurtured as such.

When a great Tibetan teacher dies, a search ensues to find the new incarnation of this released soul. Children born within a short time of the death are sought out and assessed before the new incarnation is identified.

GRANDMOTHERS AND GRANDFATHERS

Other shamans develop over a period of time, allowing the passage of life to awaken their wisdom and their unique gifts. After raising a family, many women and men become free to take the path of the healer, the seer, or the creative spirit; some become the guiding force for others within the community. These are the grandmothers and grandfathers who lovingly share the wealth of their experience. Before the advent of modern medicine, in many cultures it was the grandmothers who were the midwives; older women with their own experience of childbirth helping their daughters to bring new life into the world.

Learn from others' experience.

SHAMANIC DEATH

Many shamans awaken to their wisdom during periods of challenge, upheaval, or rapid change in their lives. In some cases it is the emergence of the true self from within that causes the upheaval, in others it appears to be external circumstances that trigger the shamanic spirit to awaken. Some people experience a shamanic death during their childhood or their teenage years, while others experience a mid-life crisis that sets them forth on a new course.

A crisis may open the door to deeper understanding.

A shamanic death can come through an illness, a period of emotional turmoil, depression, a nervous breakdown, or a near-death experience. It can come with a loss of hope, a loss of direction, or with confusion. It is as if everything that we have ever learned about life breaks down and dies, allowing our greater wisdom to emerge. Shamanic death is not essential to be a shaman, but it is a path that many have taken.

REBIRTH

Making a fresh start can be an invigorating experience.

Coming out of a period of shamanic death, there is a rebirth, a new awakening of the spirit, and a new direction begins to emerge. Many cultures have supported the process of death and rebirth by providing rituals and rites of passage for the different stages of life.

Often the newly emerged shaman is honored and respected; sought out for his or her new insights and broadened perspective on the world. The period of rebirth is a time when we remember who we truly are, cast off the fears, limitations, and negative expectations of the past, and learn to trust our intuition. It is a golden dawn where we leave behind the dark night of the soul and step out with a new awareness of personal power. Shamans often develop a true humility, one that comes with a knowledge of how extraordinary and how powerful they truly are!

THE ELEMENTS

Historically many shamanic beliefs and traditions have grown from a powerful awareness of the natural world. Before the advent of modern technology, indigenous peoples knew that to survive they needed to respect the elements and live in harmony with nature.

THE INNUA OF THE ESKIMOS

The traditional religion and culture of Eskimo peoples reflect the harsh extremes of their environment. Innuit traditions include a belief that the world is ruled by a multitude of invisible forces called *Innua*. The sea, the air, the animals, and the stones all have their *Innua*. These can become the guardians or helpers of men if given their due respect.

The Innuit divinity of the sea and the sea mammals is called Sedna. Once a beautiful maiden, this goddess is seen as hostile and is feared, a view that reflects the physical reality of the turbulent and dangerous waters that these people traditionally navigated and fished for their survival.

INDIANS OF THE PLAINS AND FORESTS

This belief in the invisible forces or spirits of the natural world is a universal one. Other indigenous peoples of North America, such as the Indians of the plains, hold a belief in a Great Spirit that is the breath of the divine within all things. The Great Spirit can be honored and worshipped by honoring and learning from the spirits of the natural world, the sun, the moon, the winds, the rain, thunder, and lightning as well as the animals, birds, plants, and stones.

The Algonquins and Iroquois peoples of the North American forests also hold a belief in a great spirit and observe that everything in nature is inhabited by a mysterious power. The Algonquins call this power *Manitou* and the Iroquois call it *Orenda*.

The natural world has much to teach us.

COMMUNING WITH THE SPIRITS

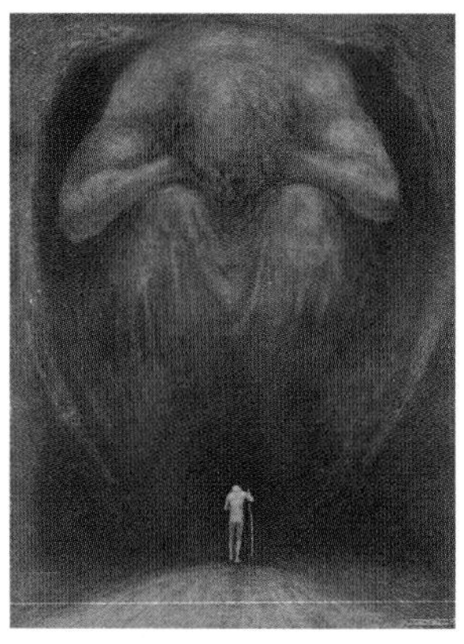

Personal heritage can enrich and guide our lives.

It is the shaman's job to communicate with the spirit world, giving respect to the spirit of the ancestors, as well as to live in harmony with nature. The ancestors are the spirits of the people who have gone before us; they are our great-grandparents who have lived in the world, gaining the knowledge and awareness that we are now here to learn, before passing over into the invisible realms.

The knowledge of the ancestors can be given to us through our race memories, our genetic heritage that is contained within the cells of our bodies, and through direct, "mediumistic" communication. Some shamans develop a close relationship with one or more ancestral spirits who operate as guides to teach creative and healing skills, as well as bringing information that will aid survival or spiritual growth.

ANIMAL SPIRITS

Traditionally, shamans studied the ways of the animals that were indigenous to their lands. Animals were seen as having a purity of purpose that could teach human beings much about their own spiritual potential. Sometimes whole tribes or clans of people would associate with the qualities of a particular animal, and individual shamans would have specific animal spirits as guides.

During trance states induced by meditation or sacred ritual the shaman would contact his or her power animal and journey with it through the inner planes. These power animals would literally or symbolically pass on important insights about the shaman's own nature, the nature of the person seeking healing or counsel, and the needs of the community.

THE ROLES OF THE SHAMAN

The first medicines were herbal.

The roles of the shaman are numerous and diverse but they all serve a greater purpose. Through his or her chosen pathways, the shaman can build bridges between the physical and non-physical, can serve the earth, serve humanity, and touch the divine so that healing may occur.

The shaman is, first and foremost, a healer. In all cultures there are natural healing traditions. Modern medicine grew from the skill of the herbalist, the medicine man or woman, the white witch, and the faith healer. Medical science has made many advances, treatments have been developed that at one time would have been considered to be miraculous, but it has also lost areas of sacred knowledge and human awareness that give the process of healing its meaning.

As healers, shamans learn from nature.

SACRED BALANCE

Healing is needed when someone or something has become out of balance. It is the shaman's job to find that balance within himself or herself and then help to restore it to others. The Chinese symbol of yin and yang is a powerful totem of balance. The areas of white and black are evenly distributed and there is a little of each that resides within the other.

Chinese medicine has sought to maintain that balance of yin and yang for thousands of years. Chinese doctors work with energetic meridians or subtle circuits of energy that pass through and around the physical body. When an imbalance occurs, these meridians become blocked or distorted and disease is able to take hold. The original imbalance can be physical, mental, emotional, or spiritual. A poor diet, unexpressed emotions, imbalance within the environment, and numerous other causes can create a disturbance that may in time manifest itself as a disease.

THE PERFORMER

In many cultures the shaman was the actor or performer whose creativity helped other people to find meaning in common experiences, powerful feelings, and the rites of passage through which we all must travel. Shamans directly interpreted the significant events of life, such as birth, death, puberty, marriage, and spiritual awakenings, through mime, dance, ritual, and song. Some would use masks, costumes, body paint, and movements or gestures that had been passed down from generation to generation.

The Kathakali dancers of Kerala in southern India undergo a rigorous training from childhood to ensure that they have the skill and suppleness of gesture to embody deities and demons in the legends that they re-enact. Their make-up and costumes alone take hours to apply and during their performance they often become one with the character they are playing.

A shaman in bird costume performs a traditional ritual.

THE SACRED DRUM

Drumming into awareness.

Finno-Ugric, Native American, African, and Asian cultures all used drums as a key element of ritual, ceremony, and performance. The Finno-Ugric race comprises many tribes that inhabit an expanse of Europe and Asia from Finland to Siberia. One sub-group, the Lapps, relied upon their "magic drums" or quodbas to keep time as they chanted their sacred exorcisms.

The beating of the drum was used by shamans to send themselves, and others participating with them in sacred ceremonies, into states of ecstatic awareness. Amongst the Samoyed peoples of Siberia only the most advanced shamans or sorcerers used sacred drums and invoked spirits.

Native Americans associated the drum with the beating of a heart and with the natural rhythm of Mother Earth. The drums used in ceremonies created a collective consciousness amongst participants for the purposes of healing, celebration, spiritual journeying, and prayer.

THE FOOL

The shaman could also be the fool, the clown, or the court jester; using skill, ingenuity, and humor to entertain or to diffuse potentially dangerous situations. In some circumstances, the fool could speak the truth when others were too frightened to do so. The grinning simplicity of the fool was great protection for a wise shaman, whose cleverness might otherwise have been seen as a threat.

The Fool in Shakespeare's play *King Lear* is a character who foresees the tragedy of the drama that unfolds and does his best to warn his master, the King, of the events to come:

FOOL: Nuncle, give me an egg and I'll give thee two crowns.

LEAR: What two crowns shall they be?

FOOL: Why, after I have cut the egg in the middle and eat up the meat, the two crowns of the egg. When thy clovest thy crown in the middle, and gavest away both parts, thou borest thine ass on thy back o'er the dirt: thou hadst little wit in thy bald crown when thou gavest thy golden one away.

THE OBSERVER

A successful fool always had keen powers of observation. By observing a series of events and by noticing the actions, feelings, and reactions of other people as well as listening to their words, a clever shaman may be able to predict the outcome of many situations.

Some shamans have the power of "invisibility." They are able to blend into the background or become one of the crowd so that they can monitor events unnoticed and unhampered by others. This is an important skill for us all to learn when we are feeling vulnerable or when we wish to bring healing or support to another without attracting unwanted attention.

There are also times when it is valuable to turn this skill upside-down and become highly visible. The fool can use colorful costumes, jokes, and tricks to create a diversion when there is someone or something that needs protection.

The Fool entertains King Lear

THE SACRED ARTIST

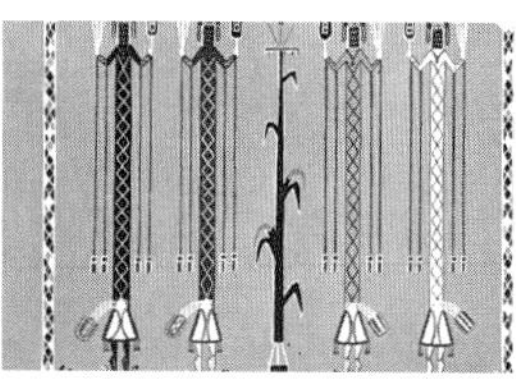

The hail chant of the Navajo Thunder People.

Shamanic traditions included the use of sacred art in ceremonies of healing and as a bridge between the physical and non-physical worlds. The Navajo people, who now chiefly reside in the south-western states of the USA, have practices of sand painting that have been passed down from generation to generation.

Sand painting is a lifetime's work; the artist becomes skilled at locating colored rock from the canyons and gullies of the region and at grinding it into a fine powder that can be precisely sprinkled into sacred images. The religious significance of many symbols makes them too important for the Navajo to share with the outside world; however, the colors and images are chosen to bring balance to the person or situation that requires healing. Once the healing ceremony is complete, the painting is destroyed and the sand returned to the earth to complete the creative cycle.

HEALING AND CREATIVITY

Tibetan Buddhists, too, have a tradition of sand painting. Tibetan monks perform many rituals of healing that include sacred dance, music, and chanting as well as sand painting. Their rituals are carefully practiced to attract a "medicine buddha" or to cleanse the environment. Like the Navajo, Tibetan monks destroy their sand paintings once their ceremony or purpose has been completed.

The creative act is in itself a powerful force for healing and transformation. Great artists, musicians, and poets have talked about receiving inspiration from a "muse" or spirit guide as they work; many describe losing themselves in the joy and passion of their creativity. Creativity helps us to transcend the normal, physical reality of our daily lives and touch the divine. In doing so we bring healing to ourselves and to those who are influenced by our work.

Sand paintings have religious significance for many peoples.

THE SEER

Many shamans were the seers, the visionaries, and the psychics whose knowledge of human nature, intuition, and powers of divination were highly regarded by others. These shamans had managed to develop natural skills of clairvoyance, clair-audience, and instinctual awareness that are latent within us all.

In the Hellenistic world there were prophets or "mantics" who were visionary seers. Their visions were often interpreted by others, particularly those skilled in the arts of divination and astrology. Today many good astrologers, diviners, and card readers are also skilled psychics who use their craft as a focus for their visionary abilities.

THE INNER SENSES

Whether we are aware of it or not, many of us receive visual information through our third eye. The third eye is a subtle energy centre positioned in the middle of the forehead. It is one of the main energy centres of the Indian chakric system, which maps the points within the human anatomy where the physical and non-physical bodies meet. The third eye or brow chakra is linked with vision, intuition, higher thought, and inspiration.

The visual sense is only one way that we receive extra-sensory information. Some of us hear words in our heads or have inspired thoughts that come to us during dreams or day-dreams, others have gut instincts or can instantly detect the mood and feelings of people, environments, and situations. We may not recognize our psychic or intuitive abilities because they have always been with us and so they do not seem to be particularly different or remarkable. Focusing on our innate abilities and practicing them can allow them to grow.

Practicing our intuitive abilities
will open our third eye.

THE OUTSIDER

The shamans' capacity for clear sight often came from a unique perspective. Their ability to attain altered states of awareness gave them a bigger picture of the world, which allowed them to see beyond the daily dramas of community life. Even if they did not understand the significance of every event that occurred within the clan or tribe, they knew that each occurrence was part of a greater spiritual pattern and that everything had its meaning and purpose. In addition, the social position of the shaman often liberated them from the tasks of day-to-day survival. While being a full member of the community, the shaman could also be on the outside looking in.

For the modern shaman, the ability to develop effective visionary skills often comes from a willingness to be on the inside and the outside at the same time. We need to develop our careers, pay the bills, bring up our families, fall in love, and do a host of other normal things so that we can understand the needs and frustrations of the people whom we serve. However, we also need to learn a degree of detachment and make sure that we do not get too caught up in the events and dramas of our lives.

THE LEADER

The visionary role of the shaman often brought social and economic power. The shamans of the Tungus peoples became powerful enough to attain political prominence and leadership. Similarly the Eskimos often gave the position of leader and shaman to the same person. A mark of true leadership is a willingness to act upon one's beliefs, never expecting to send others into situations that one is not willing to experience oneself. For this reason, some of the best healers and teachers are those who have first-hand experience of the spiritual transitions that they are helping other people to make.

Shamans often make effective leaders.

YOUR INNATE SHAMANIC ABILITIES

While it is true that some are born with a strong vision of their shamanic purpose and others go through an experience at some time during their lives that brings their shamanic potential to the surface, neither scenario is essential proof of latent shamanic ability. For many people, the path of the shaman is a process that gently unfolds without the need for drama or revelation. It could be that discovering your shamanic potential is similar to gently waking up from a long sleep to discover the beauty and wonder of the day ahead.

Recognize and nurture your shamanic potential.

If you require proof of the spirit of the shaman waking within you, then look no further. You would not be reading this book if you did not have a degree of shamanic potential. There are no coincidences; everything that we read contains a message for us, if we are willing to see it.

INSTINCTS

To unleash your innate shamanic abilities it is important to find the balance between the logical, reasonable, and rational side of your personality and the instinctive, intuitive, irrational qualities that you also have. Shamans need to be aware of a full range of human emotions, to feel them, to live with them, and to draw motivation from them, as well as learning how to detach from them when they obscure the truth of a situation.

In modern times, humanity has neglected the creative power of intuition and instinct. Many of us have lost touch with our inner peace, stillness, and simplicity of purpose and we have alienated ourselves from the spirits of the natural world. To become a shaman it is important to repair this.

A shaman's storage chest.

THE VISION QUEST

Calling up an animal spirit guide.

Many shamans traditionally retreated from community life so that they could reconnect with the natural world and find places of stillness and truth that would enhance their powers of vision. These "power spots" often had an increased spiritual or electrical energy, which would stimulate their psychic senses and help the vision-seeker to journey within for inspiration and guidance. Shamans would also help others who were questing for direction in their lives by guiding them to do the same. In some cultures the seeker would fast and meditate for a few days until receiving their vision.

During a vision, the spirits of the natural world may visit the seeker, bringing protection, wisdom, and awareness, and helping them to harness their talents. The vision quest could be a time for connecting or reconnecting to special guides, who could appear in the form of an ancestor, an animal, a plant, a stone, or any other aspect of nature. It could also be a time of reconnecting to your divine purpose, remembering who you are, and what you came into the world to learn and to contribute.

A DAY OF STILLNESS

Give yourself a day of stillness and peace to be with your feelings and inner vision. If you can find a quiet spot of natural beauty where you will be safe and relatively undisturbed, do that. Alternatively, choose a day when you will be on your own at home. Minimize distractions by eating sensibly but simply, unplugging the telephone, turning off all televisions and radios, and making your environment as calm and silent as you can. Sit comfortably and spend the day breathing deeply, noticing your thoughts and impulses.

Find a place for contemplation.

CHOOSING YOUR POWER ANIMALS

While undertaking a day of stillness or shorter periods of meditation, you could ask for specific areas of support. If you are facing challenges in your life or if you have lost direction it is important to ask for the guidance you require, either out loud or in your head. You could also ask for your own personal spirit guides to reveal themselves to you, which they may do with a feeling, a thought, a sound, a fragrance, or an image revealed to your inner eye.

If you wish, you could ask for a visit from a power animal. Begin by focusing upon the animals that you particularly love. What qualities do you admire about them? What do they have to teach you? How can they help you to heal your view of the world or find new solutions to your problems? Alternatively, allow your mind to go blank and ask for an animal to be revealed to you. Often your first thoughts are sound, but as you sit longer you may have more animals come to mind or show themselves to you physically. Each visit can teach you something about your spiritual path.

THE SIGNIFICANCE OF ANIMAL SPIRITS

Many cultures invested animals with spiritual significance. In ancient Egypt, most gods and goddesses were depicted as half human and half animal, or were said to assume animal form. Goddesses such as Hathor and Isis could take the form of a cow to signify great maternal power and compassion. The sun god could assume the form of Khepri, the scarab beetle. The goddess of childbirth was called Heket, who was represented by a frog. Shamans would often invoke animal spirits to help them with ceremonies of healing and rites of passage.

Ancient Egyptian gods and goddesses were often depicted as animals.

YOUR CREATIVITY

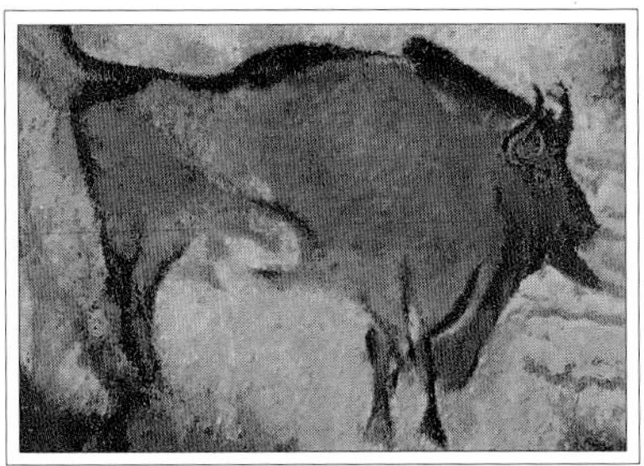

Prehistoric creative inspiration!

Awakening the shaman within you may come with awakening your creative power and ability. Many of us squash and destroy our creativity by judging it before we have given ourselves the opportunity to explore it fully. We may compare our efforts to those of other people, and we could be unwilling to engage in a creative act because we fear failure and disappointment.

The shamanic power of creativity is more concerned with the process than with the finished product. The act of creating opens up the channels to other dimensions and encourages expanded states of awareness. The creative act can also heal us of spiritual, emotional, or mental wounds and release us from self-imposed limitations.

UNLEASHING YOUR CREATIVE POWER

Pick up a pen and paper and allow yourself to write. Write about your thoughts, feelings, and experiences; find words to convey your greatest dreams and desires. It does not matter whether you write it as a diary, a poem, a story, or a song. It does not even matter if it does not make sense to begin with. Just allow yourself to write and ask your spirit guides to help you express yourself. Alternatively, you could express yourself with paints, crayons, modeling clay, fabrics, or any other medium. Remember to create first and then later decide what you would like to enhance the next time that you do this.

When painting, it can be useful to paint symbols for the areas of your life that you wish to heal. The act of symbolizing our inner wounds and placing them outside of ourselves in this way can help to transform them. Rather than holding on to our hurts it is preferable to express them and then let them go, moving on to better things.

SHAMANIC AWAKENINGS

If you feel that your shamanic nature is awakening through a period of crisis in your life, then it would be better for you to surrender to that process rather than fight it. People who have only had a passing interest in spiritual matters or who have been cynical about natural healing skills and psychic abilities often find that all of that changes when they face personal loss or illness. Our repressed instinctive nature frequently emerges when the challenges of life prove too great for our powers of reason. Many life experiences cannot be handled with logic alone; we need the expanded view that is offered to us by our intuition and by our connection to the divine, if we are going to be able to make sense of our lives and fulfil our true potential.

In astrology, the planet Pluto is associated with death and rebirth. Pluto was named after the Roman and Greek god who tricked the flower goddess, Persephone, into becoming his bride and living with him in the underworld. When Pluto is powerfully aspected to key areas of our astrological chart, it indicates a need to bring the hidden facets of our personality to the light to be transformed.

AFFIRMATIONS FOR AWAKENING YOUR UNIQUE SHAMANIC NATURE

Affirmations are declarations for regular use. With frequent repetition they can transform our thought patterns and awaken our positive potential.

MY UNIQUE SHAMANIC GIFTS
ARE NOW REVEALED TO ME

✳

IT IS SAFE TO AWAKEN MY SHAMANIC AWARENESS

✳

MY HIGHER PURPOSE NOW MANIFESTS IN MY LIFE

✳

I NOW BECOME THE SHAMAN THAT
I WAS ALWAYS CREATED TO BE

✳

I ALIGN MYSELF TO THE WISDOM
AND GOODNESS WITHIN ALL THINGS

✳

I SERVE THE HIGHEST HEALING OF ALL CONCERNED

YOUR PSYCHIC ABILITY

Many people find that as they focus upon their own spiritual growth, self-healing, and personal development their intuition naturally expands. We all have a range of psychic senses as real and as important as our five physical ones. Each of us tends to be more open and gifted in some areas and less in others, but we all have innate psychic abilities that we can develop.

You may already have clues to your psychic potential. If you are someone who is very visual, able to picture things clearly in your head, or have vivid, colorful dreams, then you may be able to awaken your clairvoyant abilities. If you are someone with acute hearing or if you are able to hear subtle words or sounds inside your head, then you may be clairaudient. If you are a good listener or are naturally drawn to bring comfort to others, then you may have latent healing skills. If you know what other people are thinking or know who is calling you when the telephone rings, then you may be telepathic.

Meditating, practicing yoga, being creative, learning to read tarot cards, singing, chanting, taking care of other people, or joining a psychic or healing development group may all help you to strengthen and increase your natural gifts.

A DECLARATION OF PSYCHIC PROTECTION AND INTENT

I now safely awaken my psychic abilities. I place the light of protection around my inner eyes, my inner ears, my capacity to receive and to know. My psychic skills blossom and expand in line with my highest good. I use them to serve the highest good of all concerned; in harmony, light, and peace.

THE WOUNDED HEALER

The shaman has often been described as the wounded healer. A wounded healer is a person who brings healing to others as a way of helping to heal his or her own wounds. If we are broken-hearted, then we may be drawn to serve others by helping them to heal their heartache. We may offer guidance that also stimulates a process of healing within ourselves. If we have survived a potentially fatal cancer, then we are ideally placed to support other people who are coming to terms with a life-changing diagnosis. In doing so we may stimulate our own unresolved feelings to emerge so that we can come to terms with them and make some new, positive decisions about our future.

It is not necessary to create wounds or problems in order to become a good shaman. Being the wounded healer is not about damaging or sabotaging our lives so that we can understand the problems of others at first hand. Instead, we need to be willing to continue healing ourselves as we follow our shamanic path and draw from the wisdom of our own personal experience. In finding our own strengths, we help other people to grow stronger. In providing strength for others, we strengthen ourselves.

AFFIRMATIONS FOR TRANSFORMING "WOUNDS" INTO STRENGTHS

AS I HEAL MYSELF I HELP TO HEAL
THE WORLD AROUND ME

*

MY LIFE'S EXPERIENCE SUPPORTS ME IN BRINGING
STRENGTH AND HOPE TO OTHERS

*

MY LIFE IS SUCCESSFUL AND FULFILLING

*

I AM ABLE TO TRANSFORM MY LIFE FOR THE BETTER

*

ALL OF MY RELATIONSHIPS ARE
HEALING RELATIONSHIPS

*

I AM GUIDED TOWARD WISDOM
AND ENLIGHTENMENT

THE STORY OF CHIRON

In Greek mythology, Chiron was a noble centaur, half man and half horse, who instructed many Greek heroes in philosophy, the arts of government, and the skills of combat, music, and healing. His pupils included Achilles and Jason. He also taught techniques for setting bones to Asclepius, son of Apollo, whose ability to heal was so profound that he could even bring the dead back to life.

Chiron is the archetypal wounded healer. In one story he was injured by Heracles, whose arrow struck Chiron in the leg, creating an unhealable wound. In an alternative tale he was pierced by a poisoned arrow while he was attempting to help another injured centaur.

Being immortal, Chiron was unable to die from his wound and so was left in a state of eternal suffering. His natural ability to bring healing to others was greatly increased by his own quest for wholeness and relief. He eventually found peace by swapping places with the tortured Prometheus; in doing so he lost his immortality and was able to die. Finally, Zeus, King of the gods, immortalized him once again as the constellation named Centaurus.

MIND AND BODY

Disharmony and disease often occur when there is a conflict between the mind and the body. Chiron, as half man and half horse, can be seen to represent the tension between the logic and reason of the mind and the instinctual nature of the body. It is the job of the shamans to negotiate a balance of mind and body within themselves, as well as to help others to find that balance. When our thoughts and feelings are in agreement with each other our spirit is free to grow.

Chiron the centaur carries a dead poet.

LIFE IS A MIRROR

The experiences that we have in our lives are often a mirror of the thoughts, beliefs, and feelings that we have inside us. Acknowledging this can allow us many opportunities to heal and to grow. If we have friends who are generous and loving toward us and who have special qualities that we admire, it is important to acknowledge that we too have wonderful qualities. Our beliefs and our attitude to life support us in making special friendships, and our qualities are reflected in the people who choose to be with us.

If, instead, we are surrounded by people who are negative, critical, or abusive, then recognizing the mirror that they hold up to us can help us to grow and change for the better. If you are always criticized by others, then perhaps you could learn to change your own beliefs and behavior about criticism. Are you ever critical of other people? Do you criticize yourself? Do you have beliefs about yourself and expectations about life that could be inviting criticism? Changing the way that you think about yourself will help to heal your shamanic wounds and transform the view that you see in the mirror.

THE MIRROR OF THE MAYANS

The Mayans of Central America and other Native American peoples taught the concept of mirroring. They knew that the mirror provided for us by others has a greater message. When we look carefully we can see that we are all one and the same, no one is greater or lesser than anyone else, we are all connected to the divine. When the children of the earth recognize their oneness, then war and conflict will end. As we heal our own wounds we help to heal the world.

TRANSMUTING POISONS

The wounded healer often has the gift of transmuting poisons. In some Native American cultures a person who lived through a snakebite was automatically invested with shamanic powers. The poison of the snakebite is a symbol for the darker side of the personality, such as the fears, the self-loathing, and the limitations of the ego that we all need to come to terms with and heal in order to grow.

A person who has learnt to love his or her dark side and bring it to the light is able to view the world with excitement and positive anticipation rather than with fear. To transmute our poisons we need to learn to think positively, come to terms with all of our feelings, and forgive the frustrations and failings of the past. Whenever we do this we awaken to a new sense of lightness and liberation.

THE SPIRITS OF HEALING

Shamans and spiritual healers have traditionally called upon spirit guides to help with the process of healing. Healing guides can be "ancestors" who teach the living how to stimulate a natural process of healing within others. The body, mind, and emotions all have their innate ability to stay healthy; when this ability becomes blocked, spiritual and energetic forms of healing can help to stimulate it again and support the whole being in regaining balance.

Some shamans and healers invoke angelic forces. Others may summon archetypal energies that have specific healing properties, such as gods and goddesses or the forces of nature. In ancient Egypt the goddess Isis was thought to have many magical healing powers. She was particularly called upon to bring healing to children and to relieve the effects of bites, scalds, and poison, particularly the venom of scorpions and snakes.

The goddess Isis standing behind the throne of Osiris.

HEALING WITH HANDS

Everyone has a natural ability to give hands-on healing. There are many different systems for giving healing but they all have a similar intention. By placing our hands on or near the person to whom we wish to give healing to, and imagining a beam of bright light passing through us, we can act as channels for healing energy. With practice we can learn to intuit the areas of the body that need additional attention and respond accordingly. Many people who do this experience feelings of heat, coldness, or tingling in their hands as the healing energy moves through them and on to the recipient. Giving healing can safely support the effectiveness of medical and complementary therapies.

ABSENT HEALING

Summon up the golden light of healing energy.

Many shamans were experts at sending distant thought. Some had the ability to communicate telepathically with their brothers and sisters, others developed the skill of reading information from a distance and sensing approaching danger or good tidings. Many more were skilled at sending absent healing, which they did when they were unable to practice their crafts face to face with the person in need of their help.

You can send absent healing by simply closing your eyes and imagining the person whom you wish to assist. See that person bathed in the bright golden light of healing energy and imagine them able to use that light to create balance within and around them. If they need protection, then see the light protecting them; if they are injured, see the light speeding up the process of repair; and if they need comforting, see the light calming them and blessing them with peace of mind. Recent scientific evidence suggests that hands-on healing, distant healing and the power of prayer really do have a marked effect on recovery rates and quality of life.

THE MODERN SHAMAN

For the contemporary shaman there is no job or role that cannot be used as a vehicle for shamanic expression and perception. Some of the greatest healers, spiritual teachers, and psychics have chosen positions that do not appear to utilize their wisdom and awareness, at some time during their lives. Any job, no matter how humble it appears to be, can give a modern shaman an opportunity to serve other people or serve the environment.

Even if your current job does not reflect your dreams and ultimate direction, you can find ways of expressing more of your special qualities while you are looking for your next step forward. If you are committed to expressing your spiritual purpose through your day-to-day activities, then your work will automatically become more satisfying. Think about your current position in life and ask yourself the questions on the opposite page.

"How can I best serve other people while I am working?"

"How can I serve my own higher purpose through my work?"

"How can my current job become more fulfilling and satisfying?"

"What can I contribute to my colleagues and clients that will make my work more creative and enjoyable?"

"How can I heal myself at this time?"

"How can I bring more healing into the world?"

It often helps to take some time to relax or meditate, asking your inner guidance to help you, and writing down or recording your answers spontaneously without judging them. If you receive important insights, then act on them. Expressing your unique shamanic purpose in your current role or job will help you to become magnetic to the opportunities that you truly desire and will move you further along your spiritual path.

CHOOSING TO BE VISIBLE

Some jobs or roles allow contemporary shamans to remain invisible so that they can practice their skills unnoticed. The world is rich with teachers, philosophers, guides, and counselors who wait at tables, program computers, build houses, cut hair, or work as receptionists. However, many shamans discover that the more they wake up to their own shamanic spirit, the more they choose professions that will allow them to express their healing skills and creative abilities. Here are some ideal positions for shamans who live and work in the modern world and who wish to become more visible.

ROLES FOR THE MODERN SHAMAN

✶ ACTOR ✶ ACUPUNCTURIST ✶ AROMATHERAPIST ✶ ARTIST ✶ ASTROLOGER ✶ CHIROPODIST ✶ COLOR THERAPIST ✶ CORPORATE TRAINER ✶ COUNSELOR ✶ DANCER ✶ DENTAL SURGEON ✶ DOCTOR ✶ ENVIRONMENTALIST ✶ EXERCISE TRAINER ✶ EXPLORER ✶ HEALER ✶ HERBALIST ✶ HOMEOPATH ✶ MASSAGE THERAPIST ✶ MEDIUM ✶ MUSICIAN ✶ NATURALIST ✶ NURSE ✶ OSTEOPATH ✶ PSYCHIC ✶ PSYCHOTHERAPIST ✶ REFLEXOLOGIST ✶ SINGER ✶ TEACHER ✶ WRITER ✶ YOGA TEACHER ✶

YOUR MOTIVES

It is often useful to examine your motives for choosing a particular career or profession. People with natural healing skills often instinctively choose jobs in mainstream medicine and health care. Good doctors and nurses tend to have healing hands, even if they do not believe in natural forms of healing.

What roles have you chosen for yourself, both at work and in your personal life? Are there links between the different jobs, roles, or activities that you have undertaken? What skills have you been required to learn and develop? If we look carefully, everything that we do can give us clues about our underlying spiritual purpose and our path to fulfilment.

Put natural healing skills to good use.

DANCING IN THE CITY

Shamans need to choose locations that best enable them to serve other people and facilitate their own spiritual growth. While it is always preferable to live close to nature, the world that we have created encourages many people to live in large urban communities. Where there are cities filled with people there is a need for urban shamans to provide inspiration, wisdom, and balance.

The urban shaman is like a flower that grows from a crack in the concrete. Both the shaman and the flower are there to remind us all of the strength, resilience, and beauty of our true nature. Some wild animals have adapted themselves to live in the city and, left unchecked, plant life still manages to survive despite the pollution and the over-development. The natural law of things is always attempting to redress the imbalance that we have created. Perhaps that is why so many people are waking up to their shamanic awareness at this time; healers and teachers are greatly needed.

THE STRESSES OF MODERN LIVING

The lives that we have chosen are often unnatural and they can cause us to lose touch with ourselves. Human beings were not built to work long hours in offices all year round or live constantly in the fast lane. We often have impossible expectations of ourselves and we may judge ourselves harshly if we do not match up to them.

It is the job of the modern shaman to remind others that we all have seasons or cycles that need to be listened to and respected. Periods of activity need to be followed by times of rest and contemplation. True success comes with responding to our true nature.

SHAMANS OF THE ENVIRONMENT

One important role for the shaman in the modern world is that of the environmentalist. The shaman has always been instrumental in helping to maintain a healthy environment. The Hopi Indians of the southwestern United States have rainmaking traditions that are passed down from generation to generation. Whenever the land was dry and parched, the rainmaker could dance and call upon the rain to replenish the earth and make the crops grow.

The modern shaman may be drawn to raise awareness about the need to take care of our environment. With uncertainty about the ozone layer, changing water tables, deforestation, pollution, and the near-extinction of many species of animal and plant life, many shamans may be called to be at the forefront of finding new solutions to global issues. If we are willing to look beyond the immediate disaster and stretch our imagination into positive expectations of the future, then our ancestors and guides can inspire us with limitless possibilities.

BECOMING A SPIRITUAL TEACHER

When we do our best to heal ourselves and follow our spiritual path we automatically become a spiritual teacher for other people. The best spiritual teachers are not always those who take center stage, although there are many inspiring people who do have a high profile. Being a teacher for ourselves and others comes with integrity, honesty, and a willingness to undertake the tasks that we have set for ourselves in this lifetime. Spiritual mastery is more concerned with the love and commitment that we take to the roles that we choose, than with the roles themselves.

True humility comes with recognizing and celebrating our special qualities and gifts without always needing to demonstrate them. In my experience it is not always those who shout the loudest about unconditional love who truly love unconditionally, nor is it always those who talk about being without ego who are most committed to moving beyond ego limitations. Wake up and acknowledge that you are special and unique but also recognize that everyone else is special too. We are all incarnations of the divine and we all have our own unique shamanic potential.

A MEDITATION FOR THE MODERN SHAMAN

Find a quiet, comfortable place to sit and relax. Have your body open, with your arms and legs uncrossed, and take long, slow, deep breaths.

Start by imagining yourself surrounded by a web of gold and silver lights that provide you with brightness and protection as you follow your shamanic path. If you do not have strong visual images when you do this, then rest assured that holding the idea is enough.

Next, invite the ancestors to bless you with their wisdom, inspiration, and protection. Picture yourself surrounded by the shamans, teachers, and healers who have lived before you and who are willing to offer you love and support as you develop. In your mind, ask them for their help and give thanks for their presence in your life.

Finally, visualize yourself traveling through the different areas of your life: see yourself at home, at work, pursuing your social life, and taking your many journeys. See yourself guided toward the people, situations, and activities that will allow you to express more of your shamanic purpose, and imagine that you are safe wherever you go. You are magnetic to spiritual growth and your highest potential for love and success.

INVOCATION

Shaman I am, timeless and free
Bridging the worlds of form and vision
Nature awakes to liberate me
My mission to serve and shatter illusion.

I ask that my gifts may bring about change
I ask for peace and evolution
I open my heart and awaken my mind
To the powers of healing and resolution.

YOUR NEXT STEPS

What are the next steps that you need to take to establish your unique shamanic gifts and apply them to the world in which you live? Others can give you guidance, support, and a wealth of ideas, but only you can decide. Meditate for a while on the following questions and take action on any inspirations that you receive:

"WHAT CAN I DO TO DEVELOP AND STRENGTHEN MY SPECIAL GIFTS?"

"WHAT CAN I DO TO SHARE MY GIFTS WITH OTHERS?"